CLEVER CUB
Gives Thanks to God

Bob Hartman
Illustrated by Steve Brown

DAVID C COOK
transforming lives together

CLEVER CUB GIVES THANKS TO GOD
Published by David C Cook
4050 Lee Vance Drive
Colorado Springs, CO 80918 U.S.A.

Integrity Music Limited, a Division of David C Cook
Brighton, East Sussex BN1 2RE, England

All Scripture paraphrases are based on the ESV® Bible (The Holy Bible, English Standard Version®),
copyright © 2001 by Crossway, a publishing ministry of Good News Publishers. Used by permission. All rights reserved.

Library of Congress Control Number 2020942530
ISBN 978-0-8307-8155-3

© 2021 Bob Hartman
Illustrations by Steve Brown. Copyright © 2021 David C Cook

The Team: Laura Derico, Stephanie Bennett, Judy Gillispie, James Hershberger
Cover Design: James Hershberger
Cover Art: Steve Brown

Printed in China
First Edition 2021

1 2 3 4 5 6 7 8 9 10

020221

"Thank You, God, for **BERRIES**!"
Mama Bear smiled.
Clever Cub scratched his nose.
He always did that
when he was thinking.

"Why are you thanking God?" asked the curious little bear.

"Because God has given us every good thing," Mama Bear said. "What do *you* want to thank God for?" she asked.

4

"Hmmm." Clever Cub thought hard.
"FLOWERS!"

"I like flowers too," Mama said.
"What else are you thankful for?"

6

"**BUNNIES**!" Clever Cub said.
"Fuzzy, **FLUFFY** bunnies—like Fred!"
Clever Cub scooped up his favorite
little bunny friend.

"But **HOW** can we give our thanks to God?" Mama asked.

"Hmmm." Clever Cub's nose crinkled up, and one brow bent down. That was his serious thinking face.

"Should I give Fred to God?" Clever Cub asked.

"Well, no, I think Fred can stay with us …
but giving what we have to God
is *one* way to say 'thanks.'"
Clever Cub hugged
Fred tight again.
"Let me tell you a story,"
Mama said.

"Long ago, when God's Son, Jesus, lived
on the earth, He had many friends.
Two of His special friends were named Peter and John.
One day, after Jesus had gone back to heaven,
Peter and John went to the temple to pray.
Imagine it. Just as they were walking up
to the big, busy temple courts—
guess what happened!"

"The temple SHOOK?" Clever Cub guessed.

"No-o-o," Mama said. "Try again."

"A flock of sheep got **LOOSE**?" Clever Cub guessed.

"No, no sheep running wild," Mama said. "I'll tell you. Peter and John saw a man being carried by his friends." Clever Cub scratched his nose. "On **PIGGYBACK**?" he asked.

"No-o-o, not exactly," Mama answered.
"They probably carried him on a cot. You see, the man couldn't walk.
He had been that way since he was born."

12

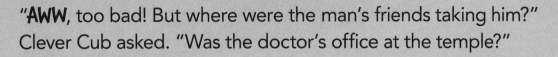

"**AWW**, too bad! But where were the man's friends taking him?" Clever Cub asked. "Was the doctor's office at the temple?"

"No-o-o, not exactly.
No doctors were able to help him back then.
His friends were taking him to one of the temple gates," Mama said. "To a gate called Beautiful."

"**O-O-O-H**, that sounds nice!" Clever Cub said.
He liked pretty things. "Was it really **BE-YOO**-tiful?"
Clever Cub imagined a gate painted like a rainbow.

13

"Hmm, yes," Mama said. "I suppose so. But mostly, it was **BUSY**.
Lots of people went in and out through that gate, to and from the temple.
The man's friends put him at that gate so he could ask for money
as all the people passed by.

14

Day after day, probably for years and years,
the man sat at that gate.
And day after day, for years and years,
the people passed on by.
Everybody knew this man from the Beautiful Gate."

Clever Cub got excited. "I know what happened next!
Peter and John passed by. But they loved Jesus,
so they gave the man **BUNCHES** of money!
And the man shouted, '**THANK YOU**!' Right?"

"No-o-o, not exactly," Mama Bear said.
"Peter and John did pass by. And they did **LOVE** Jesus.

And the man did ask for money.
But they didn't give him any money at all."

"**WHA-A-A-T**?" Clever Cub pulled his ear.
It's what he always did when he was confused.
"Not even a **BIT**?"

"No-o-o, not a bit," said Mama Bear.

"That's not very nice,"
Clever Cub said.
He didn't like this story now.
Not a **BIT**.

Mama Bear nodded. "Well, the man probably thought the same thing at first.
But Peter and John had a better gift in mind.
Peter said, 'I don't have any silver. And I don't have any gold.
But I'll give you what I do have. In the name of Jesus, stand up and walk.'"

Clever Cub looked up in surprise. "And did he??"

"He **DID!**" Mama grinned. "Peter helped the man up.
The man's feet and ankles suddenly grew strong.
And guess what he did next!"

"He said '**THANK YOU**'?" Clever Cub asked.

"No-o-o, not exactly. He didn't just *say* 'thank you.'
He went **WALKING** and **JUMPING** and **PRAISING** God—
all around the temple courts!"

"And that's how he showed he was thankful?" Clever Cub asked.

"Exactly," nodded Mama Bear.
"He thanked God with his words.
He thanked God with his praise.
But he also thanked God
by using the very thing that God had fixed.
The very gift he was thankful for."

"His **LEGS**!"
Clever Cub shouted,
leaping into the air.

"Exactly! So now, how can *you* show God you are thankful for flowers?"

"By taking care of the flowers?" Clever Cub asked.

"Exactly! Clever little bear," Mama said.
"You can water the flowers. You can watch them grow.
And you can give flowers to others and watch them smile."

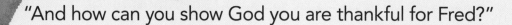

"And how can you show God you are thankful for Fred?"

"By watering him?" Clever Cub laughed and leaped into the air again.

"Well, not exactly. But yes, you can take care of Fred too. And maybe help him wash his feet," Mama Bear said.

"**EWW**. All right," Clever Cub said, wrinkling up his nose. Fred's feet were smelly! Then Clever Cub looked at his mama. "And I can give thanks for **YOU**," he said.

"By **LEAPING** and **JUMPING** and **DANCING** with you!"
And so they did—Mama Bear and Clever Cub and Fred.
They went leaping and jumping and dancing
and walking and praising God, all the way home.

For Clever Readers

Clever Cub is a curious little bear who **LOVES** to cuddle up with the Bible and learn about God! In this story, Clever Cub hears a story from the Bible that shows him new ways to give thanks to God. You can read this same lively story in Acts 3:1–10. There are so many things we can thank God for and so many ways to show our thanks!

What are you thankful for today?
How do you want to give thanks to God?